# The 'tis Bottle

Book 4
of the Trilogy
(The First Three
Books Are Being
Withheld for
Public Safety)

## Hal Goldblatt

Illustrations by Perle Goldblatt
Edited by Shawn Goldblatt

**Kravitz & Sons**
INNOVATORS IN PUBLISHING, MARKETING AND ADVERTISING

I0769700

Kravitz and Sons LLC
1301 Farmville Blvd, Suite 104
Greenville, NC 27834



Published by Kravitz and Sons LLC.

ISBN: 979-8-89639-332-0 (sc)
ISBN: 979-8-89639-331-3 (e)

Library of Congress Control Number: 2025913813

*Because of the dynamic nature of the Internet, any web addresses or links contained in this book may have changed since publication and may no longer be valid. The views expressed in this work are solely those of the author and do not necessarily reflect the views of the publisher, and the publisher hereby disclaims any responsibility for them.*

First edition: December 2012 - Hardback - limited to 100 copies.
Second edition: 2014 - Paperback
Third edition: 2025 - Paperwork

# Dedication

For Shawn
Who Has Heard This
Story 1,248,768 Times

# - Prologue -

The curtain rises and the lights come up in a comfortable living room, where an old man is sitting in a big comfortable chair reading the daily paper. Suddenly seven children rush in and excitedly ask, "Grandpa, will you tell us THE story again."

The old man chuckles and says, "Ok, gather around my children!" He reaches to his side to an end table where there is a large oversized worn book. He lifts the book but before he opens it he says…

"This is a story that happened not long ago, in a place not too far away. Like most stories it has a beginning, middle and an end". With that said, he carefully opens the book and starts to read.

# - Chapter ONE -

*Our story is about a very rich man. He was so rich he had everything he wanted and more. Being so rich he had done everything there is to do and he was bored with life. His name was Elmer J. Schmo (who makes J. Paul Getty look poor). Being bored, he called his closest advisors and asked them to come up with something new and different he could do.*

*The advisors started suggesting ideas, but alas, Elmer J. Schmo (who makes J. Paul Getty look poor) had done every single thing they suggested. For FOUR days… count them… Three, Two, One, Four, they tried to find something Elmer J. Schmo (who makes J. Paul Getty look poor) had not done.*

*Finally in desperation, one of the advisors suggested having a contest, inviting the public to suggest things that maybe, just maybe Elmer J. Schmo (who makes J. Paul Getty look poor) had not done. Also, to get people excited about the idea, a first prize of ONE MILLION dollars would be offered. This of course was pocket money to Elmer J. Schmo (who makes J. Paul Getty look poor), him being so rich and all.*

*Together they decided that they would put a FULL page advertisement in every single newspaper in the world, including the {insert the name of a local weekly paper} announcing the contest. The prize of ONE MILLION dollars would be awarded to anyone that could find something that Elmer J. Schmo (who makes J. Paul Getty look poor) had not done.*

*Elmer J. Schmo (who makes J. Paul Getty look poor) hired a staff to program a super computer with all the things he had already done so when the contest entries came they could check it without bothering him. For two weeks a team of thousands programmed the computer with everything Elmer J. Schmo (who makes*

*J. Paul Getty look poor) had done, and soon mail started coming by the truck load. Each entry was entered into the computer, but alas, Elmer J. Schmo (who makes J. Paul Getty look poor) had already done it.*

# - Chapter TWO -

Every story has to have a hero and ours is no different. The grandpa asked the kids, "Do you remember who our hero is?" They all answered together "Our Hero, Just Plain Joe". "That is correct" said the grandpa and continued to read.

Times were tough for Our Hero, Just Plain Joe. He did not have a job, nor did he have a home, nor did he have a family, nor did he have any money. Our Hero, Just Plain Joe was so poor; he did not even have a curb to fall off of. Our Hero, Just Plain Joe saw the ad in an old newspaper he was using for a blanket and it occurred to him that he might know just what Elmer J. Schmo (who makes J. Paul Getty look poor) might not have done. The problem was that Our Hero, Just Plain Joe did not have paper or a pen. He did not have postage to mail the entry. But as all heroes do, he found a way. He found an old paper bag on which he wrote with a piece of charcoal the following words: 'Have you ever collected 'tis bottles?'

Our Hero, Just Plain Joe put the paper in a mail box and hoped it would get to Elmer J. Schmo (who makes J. Paul Getty look poor). As luck would have it, the local postman figured out that the question was for Elmer J. Schmo (who makes J. Paul Getty look poor) and forwarded it to the contest address, postage due. After paying the postage, a simple clerk took the scrap of paper and entered the question into the computer.

# - Chapter THREE -

*Suddenly, bells and whistles went off. Lights started blinking and sirens started blaring. At long last they had found something that Elmer J. Schmo (who makes J. Paul Getty look poor) had not done. He had never COLLECTED 'TIS BOTTLES.*

*Of course there were a lot of questions to be answered. Who had sent the scrap of paper, what were 'tis bottles and where could they be found. Elmer J. Schmo (who makes J. Paul Getty look poor) hired the FBI and the NSA to find out who mailed the winning entry, and the CIA to answer all the questions about the 'tis bottle.*

*In less than a week the FBI was able to locate Our Hero, Just Plain Joe by DNA testing and the fact that the local postman knew who Our Hero, Just Plain Joe was. The CIA found out that there are FOUR, count them... Three, Two, One, Four 'tis bottles in the known universe.*

*The first of the 'tis bottles is located at the bottom of the Specific Ocean where it is very cold and dark.* One of the grandkids shouted out "That is the Marianas Trench". The grandpa smiled and said "very good Chaim" and continued to read; *the second of the 'tis bottles is located at the tippy top of the world's highest mountain. Another of the grandkids shouted out "That is Mount Everest". Again the grandpa smiled and said "that's right Shaina". The third 'tis bottle is located at the bottom of the coldest darkest lake... But before he could say the name, his granddaughter Shevi shouted out "That is the black Sea in Russia." Right again, he smiled and then the grandpa continued to read; the fourth 'tis bottle is located on MARS but it is guarded by the AXE MAN. Two of the grandchildren Nerya and Alex exclaimed "Not the AXE MAN! Oh no!!"*

# - Chapter FOUR -

*Elmer J. Schmo (who makes J. Paul Getty look poor) realized that they would need the world's strongest man to get the 'tis bottles so he asked his advisors how to find him. After much discussion, one of the advisors came up with an idea that pleased Elmer J. Schmo (who makes J. Paul Getty look poor). 'Why don't we have a stair climbing contest?', said the advisor.*

*Now to understand what the advisor was talking about you have to understand where Elmer J. Schmo (who makes J. Paul Getty look poor) lived. He had built a castle on top of a very tall mountain and the only way to get to his house was to climb a circular staircase around the outside of the mountain. The castle was so high up it took One Million Two Hundred Forty-Eight Thousand Seven Hundred and Sixty Eight (1,248,768) steps to reach the top.*

*Yes that is One Million Two Hundred Forty-Eight Thousand Seven Hundred and Sixty Eight (1,248,768) steps. This is a very important number in our story so it would do the reader well to learn the number. Now everyone repeat after me exclaimed the grandpa… 'One Million', 'Two Hundred Forty-Eight Thousand', and 'Seven Hundred and Sixty Eight'. Very good! A.J. and Miriam laughed and said the number again and again, just to make sure they remembered it.*

*Elmer J. Schmo (who makes J. Paul Getty look poor) put a FULL page advertisement in every single newspaper in the world, including the {insert the name of a local weekly paper} announcing the first annual stair climbing contest. A prize of ONE MILLION dollars would be awarded to the first person to climb the One Million Two Hundred Forty-Eight Thousand Seven Hundred and Sixty Eight (1,248,768) steps.*

*Anticipation was high in the Elmer J. Schmo (who makes J. Paul Getty look poor) household as the big day finally arrived. This was the social event of the year and everyone who was anyone was there. There were marching bands, floats, carnival carnies, flower girls, peddling their wears and wearing their pedals, and thousands of contestants hoping to climb the One Million Two Hundred Forty-Eight Thousand Seven Hundred and Sixty Eight (1,248,768) steps first.*

*Soon it was time to begin the race, and the starter raised the golden gun and fired the lone silver bullet; 'BANG' and they were off and climbing. Now Our Hero, Just Plain Joe, …you do remember Our Hero, Just Plain Joe, don't you? Well, he got there a bit late and started in the middle of the pack. Our Hero, Just Plain Joe started climbing and pushing and shoving people out of his way, quickly moving up the staircase until he was close to the front of the pack.*

*They climbed and climbed and climbed until finally it was just Our Hero, Just Plain Joe out in the lead. Our Hero, Just Plain Joe reached the top in a record breaking time of four days, twenty-three hours and fifty-six minutes. Our Hero, Just Plain Joe knocked on the door and immediately fainted. The butler opened the door, gave Our Hero, Just Plain Joe a glass of water and put him to bed. Our Hero, Just Plain Joe slept for FOUR days, count them… Three, Two, One, Four.*

# - Chapter FIVE -

*When Our Hero, Just Plain Joe woke up, Elmer J. Schmo (who makes J. Paul Getty look poor) was standing there waiting. Elmer J. Schmo (who makes J. Paul Getty look poor) asked Our Hero, Just Plain Joe if he knew where the 'tis bottles were located and Our Hero, Just Plain Joe told him he did. 'Well, Joe, you have TWO MILLION dollars, go get me a 'tis bottle', exclaimed Elmer J. Schmo (who makes J. Paul Getty look poor).*

*"Do you remember where the first 'tis bottle is located?" asked the grandpa. Shaina said: "The first 'tis bottle is located at the bottom of the Specific Ocean where it is very cold and dark, at the bottom of the Mariana Trench". Our Hero, Just Plain Joe knew he would need a special diving bell to go so deep so he enlisted the help of Jacques Cousteau and the United States Navy vessel, the Glomar Explorer, a deep-sea drillship platform initially built for the United States Central Intelligence Agency Special Activities Division.*

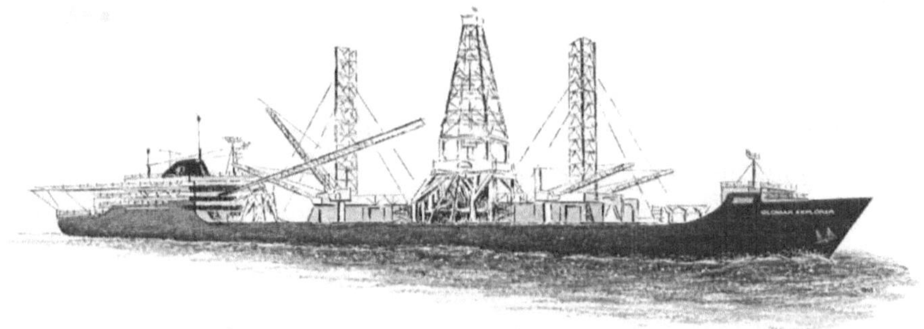

*They reached the location in the Specific Ocean and lowered Our Hero, Just Plain Joe overboard, in a special diving bell made just for him. Slowly he went down (blup!), down (blup!), down (blup!) until suddenly... there in front of him was a ten foot by twelve foot sign (because everything looks bigger underwater) that said; 'You are almost there, JOE!' Our Hero, Just Plain Joe went down (blup!), down (blup!), down (blup!) until he reached the bottom. It was very cold and very dark so he turned on his electric thermal underwear and the head lights built into the diving bell.*

*Suddenly he saw a ten foot by twelve foot sign (because everything looks bigger underwater) that said; 'Just around the corner, JOE!' Our Hero, Just Plain Joe turned the corner and there, embedded in the rock was a golden chest with a rusted padlock. Our Hero, Just Plain Joe ripped the padlock off and slowly opened the trunk. He looked inside, and there, on this UGLY green carpet (this carpet was the UGLIEST shade of green known to mankind. This UGLY green carpet made monkey vomit look good) was the 'tis bottle.*

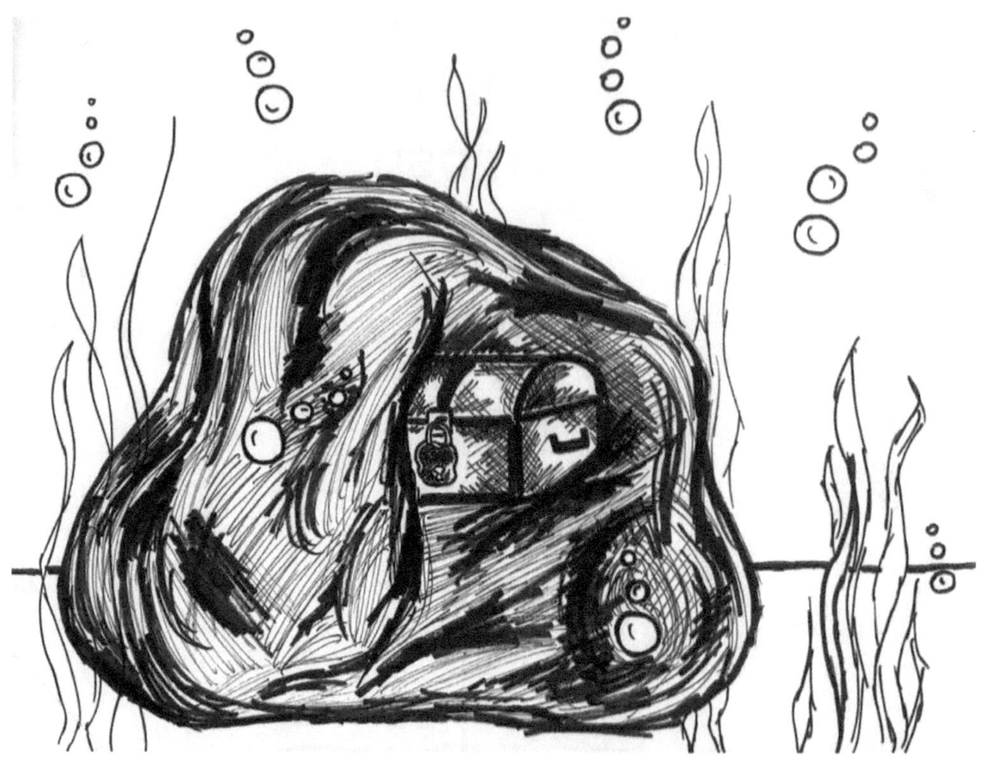

Our Hero, Just Plain Joe carefully lifted the 'tis bottle out of the chest and put it in a special harness on his left arm. Our Hero, Just Plain Joe signaled the Glomar Explorer to raise him up and slowly but steadily Our Hero, Just Plain Joe started to rise. Our Hero, Just Plain Joe went up (blup!), up (blup!), up (blup!) until suddenly, there in front of him, was a ten foot by twelve foot sign (because everything looks bigger underwater) that said; 'Look out for the GREAT WHITE SHARK, JOE!' Our Hero, Just Plain Joe signaled the Glomar Explorer to raise him more quickly.

Our Hero, Just Plain Joe went faster up (blup!), up (blup!), up (blup!) but alas the GREAT WHITE SHARK came swimming up to him and bit off his left arm, with the 'tis bottle. He finally made it to the surface; they patched him up and put him in the hospital. Our Hero, Just Plain Joe slept for FOUR days, count them… Three, Two, One, Four. Word got back to Elmer J. Schmo (who makes J. Paul Getty look poor) that Our Hero, Just Plain Joe had failed in his attempt to get the first 'tis bottle. He was sad but knew that these little setbacks happen in life.

# - Chapter SIX -

*Time passed and it was time for the SECOND annual stair climbing contest. Elmer J. Schmo (who makes J. Paul Getty look poor) put a FULL page advertisement in every single newspaper in the world, including the {insert the name of a local weekly paper} announcing the second annual stair climbing contest. A prize of ONE MILLION dollars would be awarded to the first person to climb the One Million Two Hundred Forty-Eight Thousand Seven Hundred and Sixty Eight (1,248,768) steps.*

*Anticipation was high in the Elmer J. Schmo (who makes J. Paul Getty look poor) household as the big day finally arrived. This was the social event of the decade and everyone who was anyone was there. There were marching bands, floats, carnival carnies, flower girls, peddling their wears and wearing their pedals, and thousands of contestants hoping to climb the One Million Two Hundred Forty-Eight Thousand Seven Hundred and Sixty Eight (1,248,768) steps first.*

*Soon it was time and the starter raised the golden gun and fired the lone silver bullet; 'BANG' and they were off and climbing. Our Hero, Just Plain Joe had learned his lesson in the first stair climbing contest and this time he was at the start of the pack from the beginning.*

*They climbed and climbed and pushed and shoved until finally it was just Our Hero, Just Plain Joe out in the lead. Our Hero, Just Plain Joe reached the top in a record breaking time of four days, twenty-three hours and thirty-four minutes. Our Hero, Just Plain Joe knocked on the door and immediately fainted. The butler opened the door, gave Our Hero, Just Plain Joe a glass of water and put him to bed. Our Hero, Just Plain Joe slept for FOUR days, count them… Three, Two, One, Four.*

*When Our Hero, Just Plain Joe woke up, Elmer J. Schmo (who makes J. Paul Getty look poor) was standing there waiting. Elmer J. Schmo (who makes J. Paul Getty look poor) asked Our Hero, Just Plain Joe if he knew where the second 'tis bottle was located and Our Hero, Just Plain Joe told him he did. 'Well, Joe, you have nearly THREE MILLION dollars (because he had to spend some trying to get the first 'tis bottle), go get me a 'tis bottle', exclaimed Elmer J. Schmo (who makes J. Paul Getty look poor).*

*"The second of the 'tis' bottles is where my children?", asked the grandpa and this time Alex answered, "It is located at the tippy top of the world's highest mountain, Mount Everest". The grandpa smiled and said "That is correct!" as he continued to read;*

*The second of the 'tis bottles is located at the tippy top of the world's highest mountain, Mt. Everest. Our Hero, Just Plain Joe went out and bought himself warm climbing clothing and gear. Our Hero, Just Plain Joe hired the best guides money could buy and started out climbing Mt. Everest. It was very slow at first but they continued to climb day and night, resting only when they got really, really tired.*

*The higher he climbed, the slower it went until suddenly, there in front of him was a four foot by six foot sign (because everything looks smaller in the mountains) that said; 'You are almost there, JOE!' Our Hero, Just Plain Joe climbed and climbed until he reached the top. It was very cold and the air was very hard to breath, so Our Hero, Just Plain Joe, put on his oxygen mask and turned on his electric thermal underwear.*

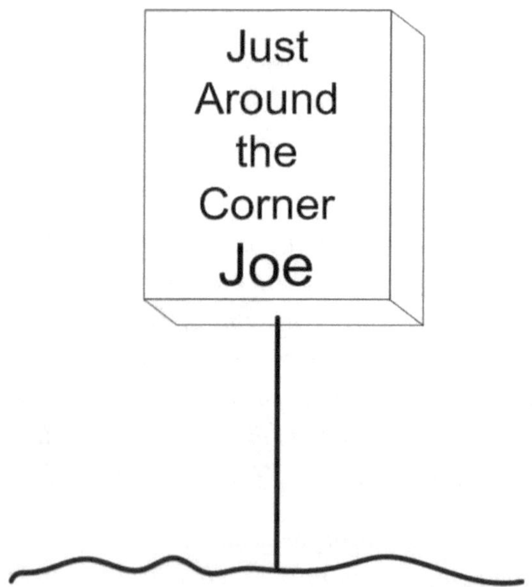


*Suddenly he saw a four foot by six foot sign (because everything looks smaller in the mountains) that said; 'Just around the corner, JOE!' Our Hero, Just Plain Joe turned the corner and there embedded in the rock was*

*a golden chest with a rusted padlock. Our Hero, Just Plain Joe ripped the padlock off the chest and slowly opened the lid. As he looked inside, there on this UGLY green carpet (this carpet was the UGLIEST shade of green known to mankind. This really UGLY green carpet made monkey vomit look good) was the 'tis bottle.*

*Our Hero, Just Plain Joe carefully lifted the 'tis bottle out and put in a special harness on his right arm.*

*Our Hero, Just Plain Joe started to go down the mountain. Suddenly there in front of him was a four foot by six foot sign (because everything looks smaller in the mountains) that said; 'Look out for the 'ABOMINABLE SNOWMAN, JOE!' Our Hero, Just Plain Joe started to run as fast as he could but alas, the Abominable Snowman caught up to him and ripped off his right arm. Alas, our Hero, Just Plain Joe fell down the rest of the mountain.*

*His guides rescued him, patched him up and put him in the hospital. Our Hero, Just Plain Joe slept for FOUR days, count them… Three, Two, One, Four. Word got back to Elmer J. Schmo (who makes J. Paul Getty look poor) that Our Hero, Just Plain Joe had failed in his attempt to get the second 'tis bottle. He was really, really sad, but knew that this would be a good reason for yet another stair climbing contest.*

# - Chapter SEVEN -

*Time passed and it was time for the THIRD annual stair climbing contest. Elmer J. Schmo (who makes J. Paul Getty look poor) put a FULL page advertisement in every single newspaper in the world, including the {insert the name of a local weekly paper} announcing the third annual stair climbing contest. A prize of ONE MILLION dollars would be awarded to the first person to climb the One Million Two Hundred Forty-Eight Thousand Seven Hundred and Sixty Eight (1,248,768) steps.*

*Anticipation was high in the Elmer J. Schmo (who makes J. Paul Getty look poor) household as the big day finally arrived. This was the social event of the century and everyone who was anyone was there. There were marching bands, floats, carnival carnies, flower girls, peddling their wears and wearing their pedals, and thousands of contestants hoping to climb the One Million Two Hundred Forty-Eight Thousand Seven Hundred and Sixty Eight (1,248,768) steps first.*

"Who can tell me how many steps", asked the grandpa. A.J. and Chaim called out together; "One Million Two Hundred Forty-Eight Thousand Seven Hundred and Sixty Eight (1,248,768) steps!" "I'm glad you're paying attention, children", he said with a smile, and then continued:

*Soon it was time and the starter raised the golden gun and fired the lone silver bullet; 'BANG' and they were off and climbing. Our Hero, Just Plain Joe had learned well from the first two stair climbing contests and since he did not have any arms to weigh him down he was at the start of the pack from the beginning, and continued to make really good time.*

*They climbed and climbed and climbed until finally it was just Our Hero, Just Plain Joe out in the lead. Our Hero, Just Plain Joe reached the top in a record breaking time of four days, twenty-three hours and four minutes. Our Hero, Just Plain Joe knocked on the door and immediately fainted. The butler opened the door, gave Our Hero, Just Plain Joe a glass of water and put him to bed. Our Hero, Just Plain Joe slept for FOUR days, count them… Three, Two, One, Four.*

*When Our Hero, Just Plain Joe woke up, Elmer J. Schmo (who makes J. Paul Getty look poor) was standing there waiting. He was a little disappointed in Joe's performance so far, but was certainly willing to give him another chance, since he did win the annual stair climbing contest again. Elmer J. Schmo (who makes J. Paul Getty look poor) asked Our Hero, Just Plain Joe if he knew where the third 'tis bottle was located and Our Hero, Just Plain Joe told him he did. 'Well, Joe, you have nearly FOUR (count them… Three, Two, One, Four) MILLION dollars (because he had to spend some of it on equipment to go after the previous two 'tis bottles), go get me a 'tis bottle', exclaimed Elmer J. Schmo (who makes J. Paul Getty look poor).*

"The third of the 'tis' bottles is where my children?", asked the grandpa and this time Miriam answered, "It is located at the bottom of the coldest darkest lake, which is the Black Sea in Russia." The grandpa smiled and said "That is right again!" as he continued to read;

*Our Hero, Just Plain Joe knew he would need the special diving bell again to go so deep so he enlisted the help of Jacques Cousteau and the United States Navy vessel the Glomar Explorer, a deep-sea drillship platform initially built for the United States Central Intelligence Agency Special Activities Division. They refitted the deep-sea drillship platform and diving bell for fresh water and off they went to the Black Sea in Russia.*

*They reached the location in the Black Sea and lowered Our Hero, Just Plain Joe overboard in a special diving bell made for him. Slowly he went down (blup!), down (blup!), down (blup!) until suddenly there in front of him was a ten foot by twelve foot sign (because everything looks bigger underwater) that said; 'You are almost there, JOE!' Our Hero, Just Plain Joe went down (blup!), down (blup!), down (blup!) until he reached the bottom. It was very cold and very dark so he turned on his electric thermal underwear and the head lights built into the diving bell.*

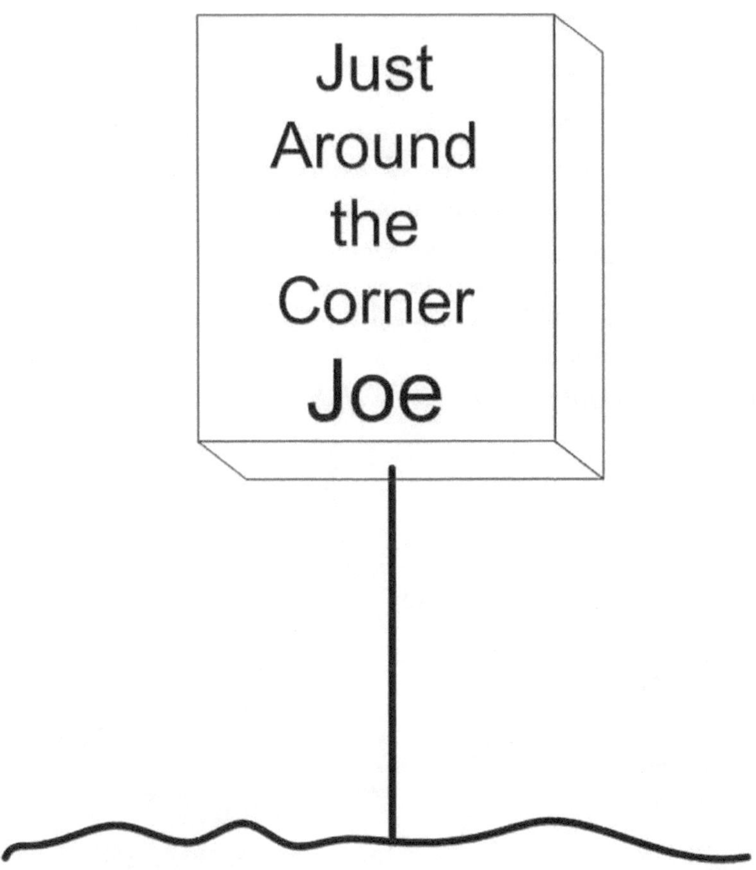


*Suddenly he saw a ten foot by twelve foot sign (because everything looks bigger underwater) that said; 'Just around the corner, JOE!' Our Hero, Just Plain Joe turned the corner and there embedded in the rock was a golden chest with a rusted padlock. Our Hero, Just Plain Joe kicked the padlock off the chest and slowly opened the lid. As he looked inside, there on this UGLY green carpet (this carpet was really the UGLIEST shade of green known to mankind. This disgusting UGLY green carpet made monkey vomit look good) was the 'tis bottle.*

*Our Hero, Just Plain Joe carefully lifted the 'tis bottle out and put in a special harness on his right leg. Our Hero, Just Plain Joe signaled the Glomar Explorer to raise him up and slowly but steadily Our Hero, Just Plain Joe started to rise. Our Hero, Just Plain Joe went up (blup!), up (blup!), up (blup!) until suddenly there in front of him was a ten foot by twelve foot sign (because everything looks bigger underwater) that said;*

*'Look out for the 'LOCH NESS MONSTER, JOE!' Our Hero, Just Plain Joe signaled the Glomar Explorer to raise him quickly.*

*Our Hero, Just Plain Joe went faster up (blup!), up (blup!), up (blup!) but alas the same GREAT WHITE SHARK bit off is right leg with the 'tis bottle. You might be asking yourself, what happened to the Loch Ness Monster as the sign warned? Loch Ness is in Scotland, not Russia for one thing and they're still not sure the monster even exists for another. In the meantime, the Great White Shark was able to swim through a tunnel to get to Our Hero, Just Plain Joe. After just one bite (okay, one arm), he liked Joe so much he just want more and more of the same flesh.*

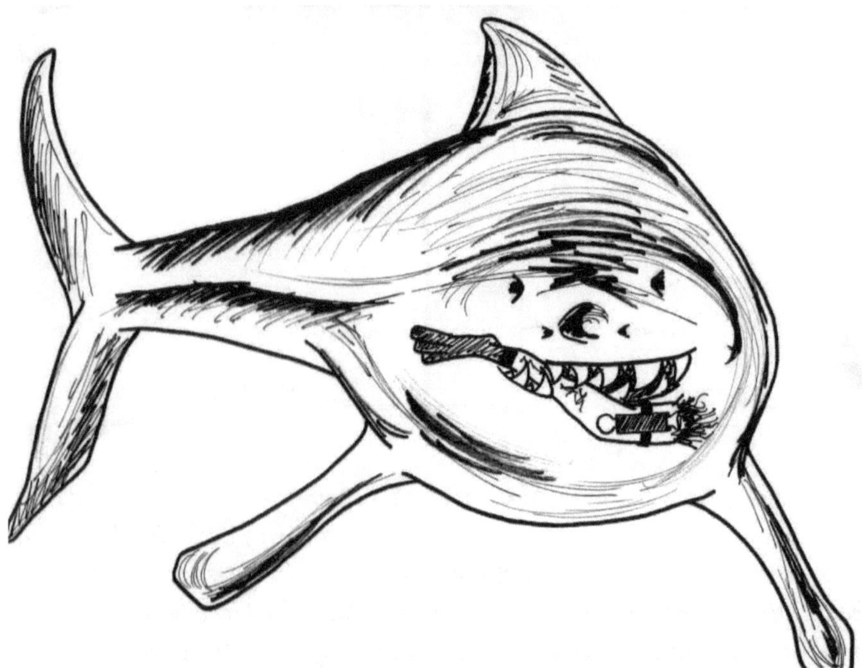

*He finally made it to the surface; they patched him up and put him in the hospital. Our Hero, Just Plain Joe slept for FOUR days, count them… Three, Two, One, Four. Word got back to Elmer J. Schmo (who makes J. Paul Getty look poor) that Our Hero, Just Plain Joe had failed in his attempt to get the third 'tis bottle. Now Elmer J. Schmo (who makes J. Paul Getty look poor) was getting a little worried and was very, very sad, but was able to look at the bright side and see that this was a great opportunity to hold yet another stair climbing contest.*

# - Chapter EIGHT -

*Time passed and it was time for the FOURTH annual stair climbing contest. Elmer J. Schmo (who makes J. Paul Getty look poor) put a FULL page advertisement in every single newspaper in the world, including the {insert the name of a local weekly paper} announcing the fourth annual stair climbing contest. A prize of ONE MILLION dollars would be awarded to the first person to climb the One Million Two Hundred Forty-Eight Thousand Seven Hundred and Sixty Eight (1,248,768) steps.*

*Anticipation was high in the Elmer J. Schmo (who makes J. Paul Getty look poor) household as the big day finally arrived. This was the social event of the millennium and everyone who was anyone was there. There were marching bands, floats, carnival carnies, flower girls, peddling their wears and wearing their pedals, and thousands of contestants hoping to climb the One Million Two Hundred Forty-Eight Thousand Seven Hundred and Sixty Eight (1,248,768) steps first.*

*Soon it was time and the starter raised the golden gun and fired the lone silver bullet 'BANG' and they were off and climbing. Our Hero, Just Plain Joe had learned well from the first three stair climbing contests but since he did not have any arms to weigh him down and only one leg, he had to learn how to hop up stairs.*

*They climbed and climbed and climbed and Our Hero, Just Plain Joe hopped and hopped and hopped until finally it was just Our Hero, Just Plain Joe out in the lead. Our Hero, Just Plain Joe reached the top in a not so record breaking time of four days, twenty-three hours and Sixty-four minutes. Our Hero, Just Plain Joe knocked on the door and immediately fainted. The butler opened the door, gave Our Hero, Just Plain Joe a glass of water and put him to bed. Our Hero, Just Plain Joe slept for FOUR days, count them... Three, Two, One, Four.*

*When Our Hero, Just Plain Joe woke up, Elmer J. Schmo (who makes J. Paul Getty look poor) was standing there waiting. Elmer J. Schmo (who makes J. Paul Getty look poor) asked Our Hero, Just Plain Joe if he knew where the fourth 'tis bottle was located and Our Hero, Just Plain Joe told him he did. 'Well, Joe, you have nearly FIVE MILLION dollars (because he had to spend some of it on the equipment he needed to try for the first three 'tis bottles), go get me a 'tis bottle. This is your last chance', exclaimed Elmer J. Schmo (who makes J. Paul Getty look poor)."You can't fail me this time!!"*

# - Chapter NINE -

"Who can remember where the fourth 'tis bottle is located?" grandpa asked. Nerya answered, "I remember it's on Mars…but it's guarded by the really scary AXE MAN!"

*The fourth 'tis bottle is located on MARS but it is guarded by the AXE MAN, so Our Hero, Just Plain Joe enlisted the help of CALTECH and NASA to build him a space ship that he could fly with just his toes and nose and a special powerful laser beam that they installed between the front two teeth of Our Hero, Just Plain Joe that he could aim and fire with his tongue.*

*Our Hero, Just Plain Joe took off and flew to Mars in his space ship. The trip to Mars took two years so Elmer J. Schmo (who makes J. Paul Getty look poor) suspended the annual stair climbing contest to give Our Hero, Just Plain Joe the time needed to get the last of the 'tis bottles. Our Hero, Just Plain Joe carefully flew the space ship using the toes of his left foot "(oh what a great name for a movie 'My Left Foot', no it will never amount to anything, but I digress)" and his nose.*

*Our Hero, Just Plain Joe finally reaches Mars and lands the space ship. He climbs into his special space suit made for him without arms and only his Left Leg. Out of the air lock Our Hero, Just Plain Joe goes and hops and hops and hops until suddenly there in front of him was a six foot by eight foot sign (because everything looks normal on Mars) that said; 'You are almost there, JOE!' Our Hero, Just Plain Joe hopped and hopped and hopped some more until suddenly he saw a six foot by eight foot sign (because everything looks normal on Mars) that said; 'Just around the corner, JOE!'*

Our Hero, Just Plain Joe turned the corner and there embedded in the rock, was FOUR, count them… Three, Two, One, Four, silver bullets… next to a golden chest with a rusted padlock. Our Hero, Just Plain Joe shot the padlock off with the laser between his two front teeth and slowly opened the lid. As he looked inside, there on this UGLY green carpet (this carpet was the UGLIEST shade of green known to mankind. This was such an UGLY green carpet that it made monkey vomit look good) was the last 'tis bottle.

Our Hero, Just Plain Joe carefully lifted the 'tis bottle out of the chest with his teeth and put in a special harness on his left leg. Our Hero, Just Plain Joe started to hop back to the space ship. Then, suddenly there in front of him was a six foot by eight foot sign (because everything looks normal on Mars) that said; 'Look out for the 'AXE MAN, JOE!'

Our Hero, Just Plain Joe turns and there towering over him at a height of twelve feet, six and three quarter inches is… the AXE MAN. The axe he is carrying is huge axe ("you might ask, how huge it is? The answer to that question would be very huge indeed"). Our Hero, Just Plain Joe takes careful aim with his laser beam and fires.

Our Hero, Just Plain Joe's aim is perfect and with one blast right between the three eyes of the Axe Man, he is dead. The Axe Man stands still for a moment and then starts to fall… towards Our Hero, Just Plain Joe. Our Hero, Just Plain Joe hops and hops and hops as fast as he can to get out of the way, but alas, the Axe Man's axe falls and cuts off Our Hero, Just Plain Joe's left leg.

Our Hero, Just Plain Joe manages to drag his severed left leg to the space ship and patches himself up. Our Hero, Just Plain Joe slept for FOUR days, count them… Three, Two, One, Four. Word got back to Elmer J. Schmo (who makes J. Paul Getty look poor) that Our Hero, Just Plain Joe had finally succeeded in his attempt to get the last 'tis bottle. Elmer J. Schmo (who makes J. Paul Getty look poor) was understandably very happy with the news and was really anxious for Our Hero, Just Plain Joe to return, triumphantly.

# - Chapter TEN -

*Our Hero, Just Plain Joe took off and flew the space ship using just his nose but because of that it took him three years to reach Earth. Finally the big day arrived and because everyone had really missed the annual stair climbing contests, Elmer J. Schmo (who makes J. Paul Getty look poor) decided to host one final stair climbing contest.*

*Elmer J. Schmo (who makes J. Paul Getty look poor) put a FULL page advertisement in every single newspaper in the world, including the {insert the name of a local weekly paper} announcing the last stair climbing contest. A prize of ONE MILLION dollars would be awarded to the first person to climb the One Million Two Hundred Forty-Eight Thousand Seven Hundred and Sixty Eight (1,248,768) steps.*

*Anticipation was high in the Elmer J. Schmo (who makes J. Paul Getty look poor) household as the big day finally arrived. This was the social event of all time and everyone who was anyone was there. There were marching bands, floats, carnival carnies, flower girls, peddling their wears and wearing their pedals, and thousands of contestants hoping to climb the One Million Two Hundred Forty-Eight Thousand Seven Hundred and Sixty Eight (1,248,768) steps first.*

*Soon it was time and the starter raised the silver pistol and fired the lone gold bullet; 'BANG' and they were off and climbing. Our Hero, Just Plain Joe having no arms and no legs had learned how to roll his body up stairs. He also had a special harness made for the 'tis bottle to protect it as he rolled.*

*The contestants climbed and climbed and climbed and Our Hero, Just Plain Joe rolled the other contestants over, knocking them all off the stairs until finally it was just Our Hero, Just Plain Joe left. Our Hero, Just Plain Joe reached the top in a not so record breaking time of four days, twenty-three hours and Eighty-four minutes. Our Hero, Just Plain Joe knocked on the door and immediately fainted. The butler opened the door, gave Our Hero, Just Plain Joe a glass of water and put him to bed. Our Hero, Just Plain Joe slept for FOUR days, count them… Three, Two, One, Four.*

# - Chapter ELEVEN -

*When Our Hero, Just Plain Joe woke up, Elmer J. Schmo (who makes J. Paul Getty look poor) was standing there waiting. Elmer J. Schmo (who makes J. Paul Getty look poor) asked Our Hero, Just Plain Joe, "where is the 'tis bottle?" Carefully, the butler unfastened the harness that Our Hero, Just Plain Joe was wearing and gently gave the 'tis bottle to Elmer J. Schmo (who makes J. Paul Getty look poor).*

*Elmer J. Schmo (who makes J. Paul Getty look poor) admired the bottle. It was truly beautiful. But Our Hero, Just Plain Joe asked Elmer J. Schmo (who makes J. Paul Getty look poor); "whatever is it good for. What is the purpose of the 'tis bottle, anyway?" Elmer*

*J. Schmo (who makes J. Paul Getty look poor) didn't answer immediately. Instead, he walked over to a wall of books and carefully started pulling books in a special order that only he knew.*

*Elmer J. Schmo (who makes J. Paul Getty look poor) pulled the third book from the fourth shelf, the seventh book from the fifth shelf, the ninth book from the first shelf and on and on and on. For FOUR days, count them… Three, Two, One, Four Elmer J. Schmo (who makes J. Paul Getty look poor) pulled books until finally the book shelves parted and started to open revealing a huge room full of all kinds of treasures.*

*Elmer J. Schmo (who makes J. Paul Getty look poor) walked to the center of the treasure room and there was a huge safe with many dials. Elmer J. Schmo (who makes J. Paul Getty look poor) turned one dial and then another and then another until the safe finally opened. The safe contained bottles of all shapes and colors. There on the top shelf was a space just the size of the 'tis bottle.*

*Carefully Elmer J. Schmo (who makes J. Paul Getty look poor) placed the 'tis bottle into the space and admired the collection. Our Hero, Just Plain Joe commented that they looked nice, but what practical use were they. Elmer J. Schmo (who makes J. Paul Getty look poor) reached to the top of the safe and took down a tiny glass hammer.*

*Elmer J. Schmo (who makes J. Paul Getty look poor) told Our Hero, Just Plain Joe that there is an ancient art form in where one can make music by tapping on glass bottles with a glass hammer and each bottle will form a different note creating the music to any song you desire.*

*With that said, Elmer J. Schmo (who makes J. Paul Getty look poor) proceeded to play the music to his favorite song…"My country 'tis….*

# The End

# - Postscript -

In the summer of 1972, I was a counselor for the Long Beach Jewish Community Center's travel camp. We went to the Grand Canyon and then south to Prescott, Arizona where we visited the overnight camp of the Phoenix Jewish Community Center's Camp.

It was late at night, and the senior counselors were gathered around a campfire when someone told the story of the 'tis bottle. The entire story took less than five minutes and everyone had a good laugh. I repeated the story the next day to our campers but added a few more details.

Over the last forty years I have added details each time I told the story and this writing is no different. I have decided to write it down on this, its fortieth anniversary. Following is a close rendition of the original version of the story I heard at that campfire…

Once upon a time, there was a fellow who was down on his luck, and as he was looking through the cla  "tis bottle."

Having nothing to lose, he calls the man who placed the ad.

"I absolutely must have this bottle, and there are only three surviving in the world," the wealthy man tells him, "one is in the heart of the deepest jungle, one is at the bottom of the coldest, darkest sea, and one is at the top of the highest mountain. I will pay your expenses for however long it takes to bring me one of these bottles, as well as giving you the ten million."

Being an adventurous fellow, he decides to accept the offer.

First, he gathers a retinue of guides and hunters to go with him into the jungle. He studies for months to prepare, and when he is ready to survive, he sets out to get the bottle.

Into the jungle he goes, and after many close calls, and much loss of life, he finds the bottle. As he is on his way out of the jungle with the bottle well packed and padded, he is attacked by wild animals, and not only is he badly mauled, but the box with the tis bottle goes flying, and box and bottle shatter.

It takes some time for him to recover from his injuries, but when he's well enough, he begins preparations to retrieve the bottle at the bottom of the sea. He takes diving lessons, hires the newest and best deep-sea diving equipment and crew, and takes to the sea.

With little trouble, they managed to get the bottle, but on the way up, they are attacked by sharks, and have to rush to the surface. In the hurry, the fellow not only gets the bends, but the bottle falls and breaks on the deck. More time in the hospital. Later, recovering slowly, he's more determined than ever to get the third and final bottle.

He spends over a year learning mountain climbing and survival, becoming accustomed to low oxygen and heights, and planning the ultimate shatter-proof container for the bottle. He hires a crew of experienced guides and begins his climb.

By the time they reach the top, they're low on supplies, weak, and frostbitten, but he will not give up. The bottle is packed and secured, and the group begins the descent.

When they reach the bottom of the mountain, the fellow again has to spend time in the hospital recovering from his injuries, but he keeps the bottle with him and in sight at all times.

Finally, he's ready to present it to the wealthy man and collect his reward.

He goes to the wealthy man's house, and carefully unpacks the tis bottle and hands it over.

The wealthy man inspects it joyfully, and hands the fellow a check for ten million dollars. "Thank you and good day, sir," he says, dismissing the fellow.

"Wait!" the fellow cries, " I was attacked by wild animals, suffered the bends, and lost fingers and toes for this bottle. I've spent years looking for it, and almost as long in the hospital from trying to get it. Aren't you going to tell me why it's so precious and what it's for?"

"Um, it's a little embarrassing, actually. Why don't you just take the money and go?"

"I'm not leaving here until you tell me what this bottle is for!" shouts the fellow.

With a sigh, the wealthy man motions for the fellow to follow him. They go into the back of the house, and the wealthy man presses a hidden button to reveal a secret door. Behind the door is a small room with another door, behind a strong gate.

The wealthy man unlocks the gate, unlocks the door, and opens the heavy vault door behind it with a combination.

Inside the vault are thousands of bottles lined up neatly, wall to wall and floor to ceiling, with one vacant spot labeled "tis".

Gently the man places the bottle in its spot, and declares "There you go."

"Oh, come on," the fellow replies. "There has to be more to it than that."

With a sigh, the man picks up a delicate, padded mallet that hangs nearby and gently begins striking the bottles, and a tune emerges. "My Country, 'tis of thee. . ."